D1346092

FOG LANE SCHOOL
And The
GREAT RACING CAR
DISASTER

FOG LANE SCHOOL
And The
GREAT RACING CAR
DISASTER

by

John Cunliffe

Illustrations by Andrew Tiffen

ANDRE DEUTSCH

First published in 1988 by
André Deutsch Limited
105–106 Great Russell Street, London WC1B 3LJ

British Library Cataloguing in Publication Data

Cunliffe, John
 Fog Lane School and the great racing car
 disaster.
 I. Title II. Tiffen, Andrew
 823'.914[J] PZ7

 ISBN 0 233 98195 0

Phototypeset by AKM Associates (UK) Ltd
Ajmal House, Hayes Road, Southall, London

Printed in Great Britain by
WBC Print Limited

CONTENTS

1
Sir's New Project

We have a lot of laughs in Class Four. I hardly know where to begin. Shall I tell you about the time Mark set fire to Sir's trousers? Or the time Linda lost her knickers? Or . . . I know, I'll start with the time Don and his mates built a racing-car. Nobody will ever forget that in our school, least of all our Sir. He nearly murdered Don that time.

It started with the Project. Sir came in one Monday morning with two big boxes of books, and all these new

folders, and rolled-up charts, and coloured card, and god knows what else. Alice and Linda went running up to his car, the way they always do, talking posh.

"Can we help, Sir? Can we carry anything?"

"Oh, thank you, girls. That's very kind of you," said Sir, all smarmy.

They always fooled him, every time. Anyway, they went staggering in with all this stuff, and Don and his mates are round the corner stuffing themselves with crisps. They had at least three bags each, but they notice what's going on all right. They never miss anything, you can be sure of that.

"See that?" says Don. "You know what that means. Work, and plenty of it. Sir's been off at the weekend, in that posh place they go to. Him and Miss Rogers. Don't you remember? He was on about it last week. 'Teachers have to go to school, as well,' he says. 'We go on learning all our lives.' He's been planning work for us all weekend."

"Him and Miss Rogers?" says Darren, grinning. "Aye aye!"

"One-track mind," says Mark.

"Never mind that," says Don. "Give us another crisp. Listen to what I'm telling you. You can bet it'll be a project, and it's nowt to laugh about. We'd better be ready for him."

They drifted off down the street to the sweet-shop where they treated themselves to a large bar of milk chocolate and a packet of chewy fruits each. They came out with their heads close together. You could tell a mile off that they were up to no good.

All this time, Linda and Alice were helping Sir in the classroom. I nipped in, pretending to look for my pencil-case, to see what was going on. They were putting Sir's charts up all over the walls. They were spreading books out on the tables. They were mixing paints and cutting card. There was a big box marked, "WRITING PAPER", and a new set of orange exercise-books. As Don said, it looked bad, very bad.

Don came back from the sweet-shop and tried to slip in, but Sir threw him out smartish. Then he threw me out, and we had to stand in the rain till the bell went.

There was the usual mad rush when the bell went, because everybody wanted to get out of the rain. There were lots of "Ooooohs," and "Aaaaaahs," as the others pushed in, goggling at Sir's new displays. Don managed to knock a table of library-books over, by accident on purpose, then Mark walked through the middle of the books in his muddy boots. Alice was still mixing powder-paint, and Darren pushed her arm so she spilled blue paint all down her new skirt. Then she hit him over the head with a tin of paint, and Sir waded in and stopped them and shouted to everyone to sit down and shut up. The day had started.

We got through register and assembly with no more disasters, and then Sir had us sitting on the carpet in the book-corner to tell us all about his wonderful new project. Don and Darren and Mark were sitting at the back pulling Naseem's hair, and Naseem was giving them each a jab in the leg with her new pencil. Then they started farting to make everybody laugh, but Sir soon had

them at the front, with a page of lines each for playtime.
That left Jimmy, pulling faces in his corner. Jimmy didn't
plan to mess things up, he just did it without thinking, and
he liked doing lines, so there wasn't much that Sir could
do about it. Jimmy sat in a corner where we weren't
supposed to see him, but he could look through a crack in
the book-case, and that made us laugh more than ever. In
the end, Sir sent Jimmy to stand outside Mrs. Foster's
room, so he never really knew what the project was all
about; not that this made much difference to Jimmy, as
he wouldn't have done it anyway. But it made a lot of
difference to our project, as you'll see later on.

We got settled down in the end, and Sir started again
about the project. There was a lot about how Good Work

would be expected from Everybody (Sir looked hard at Don and Mark and Darren when he said that) and how it would be Fun if we Got Down To It and showed a Real Interest. We were just going to find out what this Project was about, when Mrs. Peckham came in with her mop and bucket to complain about the toilets being blocked again with paper-towels, and the floors flooded, and Mark had to go out with her to unblock them, because he was caught doing it last time it happened. Then Mrs. Foster came in dragging Jimmy, yelling his head off; she wanted to know what he was doing in the Nursery sand-pit, when he should be in class. When Sir had quietened Jimmy down, and explained everything, Mrs. Foster also wanted to know who had peed in the Infants' Lego box. Everybody stared at Jimmy, and he went red in the face and

started blubbing again, and Mrs. Foster gave him a good telling-off and took him out with her. Alice was on her feet, with her hand jabbing in the air,

"Sir! Sir! It's not fair! It's not fair! Jimmy might not have done it. He always gets blamed. He always goes red when people look at him."

"All right, Alice, all right, just calm down."

This was Sir doing his cool act, the Laid Back Teacher, with his beard and red Adidas running-shoes. I've seen his sort before. You have to watch out. They get all matey, all lads and lasses together style, then they give you ten times more work than the old-fashioned sort like Miss Edwards. But Alice wouldn't be calmed down, and she finished up in tears as well, and Sir sent her to wash her face. We had lost so many kids now that Sir couldn't go on with talking about the project, so we had our milk. Don and Darren and Mark didn't look very well, and said milk made them sick. Sir smiled his knowing smile at that, but said he'd read us some funny poems till playtime. We had a good laugh at the poems, and we kept on at Sir till he read us the one that goes,

"Apple tart makes you fart,"

and we even got him to read it twice. We all felt better after that. The bell went for playtime, and the sun had come out, so everyone went out except Linda and Naseem; they stayed in to tidy up.

2
The Racing Car

We had to go in the hall for a road-safety talk after playtime, so it wasn't until after dinner that we got back to the project. Sir was looking a bit tired by now, and he wasn't having any nonsense. He even told Alice to sit down and shut up when she started on again about Jimmy. She gave him a look fit to kill, and tossed her hair over her shoulder as she plonked herself down on the carpet. She whispered to Linda, "He can sharpen his own rotten old pencils, now," and Sir pretended not to hear.

"Now, let's get on with our new project," he said brightly, and we all prepared for the worst. Jimmy still wasn't with us, as his mother had come to take him to get his hair cut, but if we waited for Jimmy we'd never get anything done. Sir went through all the pep-talk again. Luckily, my friend, Mumtaz, (most kids called him Mummy) gave me a nudge, and I woke up only just in time to find out what it was all about. Well, what it came to in the end was that you could pick your own project, and you could work with your mates in a group, or you could work on your own.

"It can't have taken him a whole weekend to think that up," said Don.

"Yes, Donald, did you have a comment we could all share?" said Sir, pleasantly.

"No, Sir. It's nowt," said Don.

You could make a model, or a display, or collect some information on the computer. At the word "model", Don looked interested, and folded his fat face into an oily smile. He liked making models, specially if he could make a mess at the same time. Then Sir wiped the smile off Don's mug with the next bit.

"I'll expect a good piece of writing from everyone, to go with the model or display."

If there's one thing Don and his pals hated it was writing. They couldn't spell for toffee, and when Sir looked at their writing-books a look of despair came over his face, and he talked about giving up teaching for good. Now Sir was saying, "I'll give you five minutes to choose your subjects and form your groups, then we'll make a list on the board."

I ask you! Five minutes to decide all that! Just like teachers. I decided to work with Mumtaz. We could do trains again; we'd done it last year, and we still had the stuff at home. We could cut the pictures out and stick them on new bits of card, and copy the writing out with all the mistakes left out, because Miss had marked it all last year, and Sir wouldn't know about that. We'd be sure to get a good mark. There was a real old din, with everybody arguing about whose group to be in, never mind what they'd do their project about, and it was more like half an hour before Sir got us all quiet again to make the list on the board.

"I bet Don picks stamps again," Mumtaz whispered to me. Don had done stamps every year, ever since he was in

Class One. You'd think he'd be sick of them by now, writing the same old stuff out every year. Of course, he'd made a group with Darren and Mark. The three of them had been huddled in the corner for a long time, heads together, like a branch of the Mafia planning a murder. They couldn't, I thought, be talking about stamps all that time. When Sir asked them their subject it came as a surprise.

"Racing cars," said Don, with that oily grin again.

"That sounds interesting," said Sir, looking hopeful. "What aspect were you thinking of? History? Design? Stories?"

"We're goin'ter build one," said Mark, with his scornful sneer.

"A model," said Darren, picking his nose.

"Don't do that, Darren, please," said Sir. "Well, that sounds really good."

He wrote, "RACING CARS" on the board.

"And how will writing come into it," he asked sweetly.

The three nudged each other and giggled, and Darren said, "We'll . . . um . . . we'll write a story . . . about racing cars."

"I'll expect some discovery-work," said Sir.

"Right on," said Darren, giving Sir a thumbs-up sign.

"Um," said Don and Mark, looking at the floor.

When the gang said they'd make a model we all thought of something that would go on the display-table. We were in for a shock. The next day, Don came to school with an enormous lump of wood balanced on his shoulder. Darren brought a pile of empty boxes, and Mark brought four wheels that looked suspiciously new, and we all guessed that he'd nicked them off somebody's pram. Sir had put a box in the classroom, marked PROJECT MATERIALS. They dumped all this stuff on top of the box, squashing it flat. When Sir told Don to move his wood, there was a sound of smashing glass that made us all jump. He'd put the end through a window! Then we had Mrs. Foster in, and Mrs. Peckham with her brushes, and the council blokes came to put a new window in, and Don nicked all their putty. They thought they'd come without it, and went all the way back to the depot for more. Don sold the putty later to the infants at 10p a lump, and they threw it at people's windows on the way home. Little Sammy, from Reception, tried to eat his. Poor kid, his mum never

gave him any breakfast, and he couldn't have school dinner since the strike. Anyway, it made him sick, and he was rushed off to hospital in case he'd swallowed any. He was there for three days. When he came back he said he'd had smashing grub, and he didn't want to come home. He asked Don if he had any more putty, but he'd sold it all by then.

That was just the start of that racing car. If Sir had only known what was coming! I heard him telling Don and friends not to worry about the broken window, but to get on regardless with their project. That was his big mistake. It was like telling King Kong to go out and have fun. Sir even allowed them to stay in at dinner-time to work on

the racing car, something they'd never been trusted to do before. I think Sir was living in a world of his own by then, letting that lot loose on their own in the classroom. I know what it was. You could tell by the way he talked to them, and stood and admired their work. After all these years of being the worst kids in the school, he thought, he had at last found something that really turned them on. They would work hard at their project, and Sir would proudly show their model off on parents' evening at the end of term. Don't tell anybody, please, but I did try to warn Sir. I knew disaster was on the way. It just wasn't like Don and his mates to please teachers. I knew they must be up to something. I got Sir on his own after school one day, and asked if I could make a suggestion.

"Look, Sir," I said, "couldn't we just drop all this project nonsense, and get back to doing our news-book and a board of sums?"

"Good heavens, no," he laughed. "The class has never worked so well before. Look, even our friends Donald, and Darren, and Mark, are working for once in their lives."

'That's what I mean, Sir," I said, but he didn't understand. It was no use. He'd just have to find out for himself.

3
The Whirlpool

Don and his mates took over a whole corner of the classroom for their racing car. They also took over most of the things that Sir had set out for us all to use for our projects. If you wanted glue, or scissors, or card, or paint, you had to go and rummage for it amongst the pile of wood and boxes in the racing car corner, as it came to be known. This led to fights until the rest of us built up a stock-pile of equipment in Sir's cupboard, and got Sir to keep it locked whenever he was out of the room. Don loved making a lot of noise, so he really enjoyed a bit of heavy hammering when the rest of us were trying to write about our projects. I went off to the school library with Mumtaz whenever I could, but you could still hear it from there. One day, Darren brought a big steel box to school, with thick wires and cables coming out of it. He had it plugged in and started up before Sir had even seen it, and there was a shower of sparks like a firework-display, and a brilliant blue light. Sir came just in time to see the school fuse-box blow up. Every single fuse had blown, and we had no lights or heating till dinner-time.

"What in heaven's name were you doing?" shouted Sir.

"It's my dad's welder," said Darren.

"My god, boy, do you want to burn the school down?" Sir was shouting so much that he was losing his voice

altogether.

"Wouldn't mind, Sir," said Darren, grinning. "I was only doing my project, Sir," he added, looking offended at Sir's fury. "We want this racing car to be really good."

"Well, I appreciate your enthusiasm," said Sir, "but you are not the only people in this school, and you will have to learn to work without wrecking everything else. You could have killed someone with that thing. Does your father know you've borrowed it?"

"No, Sir; but he lets me use it at home."

"Well you're not using it here. Understood?"

"Yes, Sir."

You know how Darren says, "Yes, Sir." You can tell it means, "Get lost, Sir," and that he's already planning his next move. Well, that's how he said it, and the rest of us decided to keep as far away from that racing car as we could whilst they were building it. Mind you, we had to admit that it was looking quite impressive. It seemed almost as big as a real racer, with a proper steering-wheel and gear-lever from Darren's dad's scrap-yard, and you could get in it and imagine you were roaring round the track at Le Mans.

Have you ever seen a picture of a whirlpool? You know how it sucks everything in and swallows it up. Well that's how it was with Don's racing car. It was a classroom whirlpool. They started with the wood and boxes they'd brought in, and most of Sir's supply of card and glue for the year had already gone into it, but that was only the start. That car had to have every fitting you could dream of. The most unlikely things began to be sucked into it. One day, when we were doing science, Sir searched through every cupboard looking for his glass funnel. If he'd taken a close look at the car's horn, he would have known where his funnel was, but it did look different covered with foil from the kitchen. (Sir never did dare tell the cook where the rest of her foil had gone. There were dozens of shiny fittings on that car.) The suction was getting too powerful for just our classroom now, and it began to take in the rest of the school. A small carpet disappeared from the top-infants' classroom, and Miss Edwards kept all the infants in the hall for three play-times, trying to get them to tell where it had gone. In the end, little Susie Mathers came up to Miss Edwards and did one of her wet whispers in her ear; "It's in a motor-car."

"In a motor-car?" said Miss Edwards. "Don't be silly, child, how can it be in a motor-car? Whose motor-car?"

But Susie clammed up and wouldn't say another word,

and got kept in at play-time for making things up, and no one ever guessed that Susie was telling the truth.

Some cushions followed the carpet; you have to have comfortable seats in a car. By now, it seemed to be a mixture of cars, and its racing car beginnings were being lost sight of. It was a cross between a grand-tourer and a jalopy. It gained a radio, and a cassette-player that looked very much like one that went missing from Rose Sutcliffe's bag in the cloakroom, but it was in a black box instead of a red one, and she couldn't prove that it was hers. There was a hidden supply of drinks behind a flap in one of the boxes. (Playtime cans of Coca-Cola went missing every day, but Sir never rumbled what was going on until the end.) It had two compasses, a thermometer, and a life-jacket. This life-jacket was really a swimming-float belonging to someone in Class Two. What was a life-jacket doing in a racing car, you may ask. You'll only get a thump if you ask Don, but the car was taking on many of the features of a boat, now. You see, Sir was nagging on about them doing some writing, and Mark had found an old project his brother had done on boats, and they thought they could copy that out. Then Darren got on about space-ships . . . you never knew what to expect from one day to another, and Sir had given up trying.

4
Blue Powder Paint

Then came the day of the great painting. Don had decided
to paint the model in deep blue paint. With a good
covering of blue, many of the parts of the car that people
might get suspicious about when it went on display at
parents' evening, would be so well disguised that no one
would know them. Don's mates were playing football that
lunch-time, so he decided to do it himself. (He never knew
I'd watched him through the window). He found two
large tins of blue powder paint in a cupboard. Then he
went to Mrs. Peckham, our caretaker, and asked to
borrow a bucket for Sir. He tipped all the powder in the
bucket, then he put it under the tap. Being Don, he liked
things to happen quickly, so he turned both taps full on.
The water comes out like a jet-plane in our school. You
have to watch it even when you're washing your hands.
But mixing powder-paint is something else. Have you
ever done it? At first, the water seems as though it doesn't
want to mix with the powder. Somehow, the powder
seems too dry for it, and the water sort of bounces off it.
You have to put a small amount in, and give it a really
good stirring with a spoon. Don had two new tins full of
the stuff, and two high-pressure jets of water. The
powder shot out of the bucket like a fountain, and into
Don's face. It covered him. It hung in big drops on his

19

eyebrows and lashes. It dripped down his fat cheeks, and off the end of his nose. I have never seen anything so funny in all my life, as this sight of a bright blue Don. I had to stuff my hanky in my mouth and roll on the grass, so that he wouldn't hear me laughing, and a dinner-lady came by and thought I was having some kind of a fit. She sent me to the toilets to splash cold water over my face and calm me down. It worked all right, and a good thing, too, as Don came running in and looked in horror at himself in the mirror. That set me off again, and he hit me and made me help to clean him up.

The next thing was that Don made me help him to paint the car. He wasn't put off at all by the accident. He couldn't get in much worse of a mess, as I pointed out, and got another thump for my trouble. I put an apron on, and helped Don. I like painting, anyway, so I didn't mind helping, and I was longing to get a close look at the car, or boat, or space-ship, or whatever it was by now. I think it had gone back to being a car, at least in Don's tiny mind. A bright blue car. I mixed the bucket of blue paint properly, and we set to work. We were slopping the paint over on the floor quite a bit, and I had an idea.

"Say, Don," I said, "why don't we stand the paint in that old water-tray? Then, if we do spill it, it won't do any harm."

"Good idea," grunted Don. "Go on then. Do it."

I dragged the empty water-tray across to where we were working. Now, all the splashes and drips went in the plastic tray, which would be easy to wash. We had painted the car all over, but Don wanted to add paste to the paint and put a second coat on, to make sure of covering all its secrets. He said the paste would add a gloss to the car, and make it waterproof. So he emptied two or three packets of paste-powder into the bucket, added more water, and we gave the mess a good stirring. He was always in a hurry to do things, and it was this that brought on disaster. He pushed past me to get at the bucket of paint, and knocked the lot over. I wasn't too worried, as the water-tray should have caught the mess. It did, so we went on painting, dipping our brushes into the water-tray instead of the bucket. We seemed to be using the paint up very quickly. One moment there was plenty of it, the next it was almost all gone! I was just wondering about this, when I heard a sound.

"Don," I said, "what's that dripping?"

We stopped and listened. Just then, the whistle went outside, and the noise in the playground stopped. Everything went quiet, except for this drip . . . drip . . . drip . . . Then a whole lot of things dawned on me at once. I was standing in something wet and sticky. There was a tide of this wet and sticky stuff moving across the classroom floor. The dripping was coming from the water-tray. All water-trays have a plug-hole, like a bath, for emptying them. The plug belonging to this water-tray was now the radiator-cap on Don's racing car. The stuff on the floor was our missing blue paint! And there was no way of stopping it.

"Quick," I said. "We'll have to get a mop."

But it was too late. The whistle had gone again. They were all coming in for afternoon school. You could hear the running of hundreds of feet along the corridors. Like the paint, there was no way we could stop them. I ran to the classroom door, leaving a blue trail. Again, I was too late. The door was pushed open and in they came. Where was Sir? This was one moment when we needed him, and he wasn't there. Only Sir could have made them wait. Before they knew it, they were paddling in our paint-and-glue mixture, spreading it everywhere. In the panic, books were knocked on the floor, and two desks went over, spilling everything in them in the paint. The kids at the front tried to push back through the door, but the

ones outside were still pushing to get in. Jimmy slipped
and fell in the paint, pulling two others down with him.
You never saw such a mess! There were shouting,
fighting, screaming and crying kids everywhere, most of
them spattered with blue paint. It looked like a battle in
one of these old SF films, with all the colours gone wrong.
Then some of the kids from Class Three came in to see
what was up, and made things still worse. Little Jenny
came with the register, and it got knocked out of her hand
into the paint, and she ran off down the corridor crying. In
the middle of all this, I was amazed to see that Don was
still painting the car, and defending it from any harm.

I don't know how long it all went on. It would have to be
the day that Sylvia Thompson's cat was stuck up a tree in
the school garden, and our Sir had gone to get a ladder to

get it down. That was why he was so late in getting back to the classroom after the whistle had gone. He turned up in the end, with the cat in his arms, purring like mad. (The cat, not Sir. Sir nearly fainted, and he was soon roaring.) He let out such a shout that the cat dug its claws into his arm, jumped down and shot out into the garden, and up to the top of the highest tree it could find.

It took hours and hours to sort everything out. We didn't do any work at all the rest of that day. (No, that was nothing to cheer about, though some silly kids did; Mrs. Foster kept us in for ten playtimes, and gave us masses of

homework, to make up.) We all had to take our clothes off and put our PE things on. Then we cleaned up our clothes and the room as well as we could. Mrs. Peckham brought buckets of hot-water and detergent and we mopped and swilled and swept for hours. There were skirts and jumpers and trousers, all patched and spotted in blue of various shades, on the radiators down every corridor of the school.

The last thing to be sorted out was Sylvia's cat. Sir had to go and borrow a longer ladder, and then the cat wouldn't come down for him. Mrs. Foster had to climb up for it, and it was past seven o'clock before they got it down, not that many of our class were there to see it, as most of us were sent to bed early for coming home with our clothes covered in blue paint.

5
"The Hystry of Moter Cars"

After that terrible day, any kid from another class who asked, laughingly, if we were feeling blue, would automatically get a good thumping. And it was a miracle that the racing car lived to see another day. Sir threatened to smash it to smithereens, but Don, for the first time ever, looked as though he would burst into tears, and begged Sir, with moist eyes, to allow the car to be kept, if only for Parents' Evening. This softened Sir's heart, and, besides, he knew that the car was all that Don's group had to show for half a term's work. Sir would look silly, too, if there was nothing to show the parents.

"And where is your written work?" said Sir, to Don, Mark, and Darren, gathered in a little huddle in front of his desk. Sir was being clever for once. He had struck them at their weakest moment!

There was a long silence, whilst all three shuffled from foot to foot. Then Don seemed to waken up, smiled as though he had just now discovered the answer to Sir's question, and said, "Lost it, Sir."

"Lost it? Lost your writing? How could you? All three of you? All at once?"

"Yes, Sir."

"Explain," said Sir, and wished at once that he hadn't, because Don set out on one of his famous explanations.

No one had ever followed him to the end of one of these stories without getting lost and hopelessly mixed up. This was why he told them. He was a whizz at doing it. He soon lost Sir, and Sir asked him to start again. He was quite glad to do this, but the story seemed quite different this time, though every bit as good. Sir asked a question that he thought would catch Don out, but it only made the story all the more complicated. Sir should have known better by now. It ended with Sir banging his desk loudly, and shouting, "That's enough of your lies. I want to see all three of you with at least five pages of writing by Friday. If you don't do it, I'll send for your parents at once, never mind waiting for Parents' Evening. Go on, now, get on with it!"

A look of pain crossed Don's face. "But sir . . ."

"No . . . no more arguing . . . back to your places, and get on with it."

The week went on more quietly now. A few grubby and crumpled pieces of paper were seen on the desks of Don, Darren and Mark. Two had drawings of space-ships on them. One had the words,

"THE HYSTRY OF MOTER CARS"

written on it, but nothing more. They went on adding bits to their car, and titivating it with pieces of foil brought from home. They spent a lot of time pretending to drive it, or fly it, or sail it, depending on how they felt. Friday came, and still no piece of writing had been done. Sir threw a temper, and sent them to Mrs. Foster. She sent them back with a toffee each. She must have thought they'd been sent to report good work. They'd eaten the

toffees by the time they came back, so there wasn't much
Sir could do about that except tell them off again. He said
they had to work over the weekend, sent a note for each
of their parents asking them to see that they did the work,
and threatened hell-fire and blue-murder if they didn't do
it.

We were all waiting for the Don gang to get into real
trouble on Monday. Nobody expected them to bring their
work in. Don would be helping in his dad's shop all
weekend. Darren would be looking after his little brothers
and sisters whilst his mum and dad went to the boozer.
Mark would be off round the shops in town with a gang
his big brother was in.

You can imagine the surprise when they all came

walking in on Monday with new folders in their hands, with a piece of work inside each one, and handed them in to Sir. He gave them a big smile, thanked them, and told them to sit down. Sir looked pleased with himself all through register and assembly, and he was specially nice to Don. He even let him off when he made rude noises during the hymn. Back in the classroom, Sir opened the folders. His smile disappeared.

"What . . . is . . . this?" he said, spacing his words out.

"Our project, sir," said Don.

"I thought your project was on racing cars?" said Sir, dangerously.

"It was," said Don, "but we changed."

"This is on stamps," said Sir.

" 'Sright," said the other two.

"What is that over there," said Sir, pointing to the car. "It looks like a car to me. It isn't a model of a postage-stamp, is it?"

A bright thought struck Don, and his face lit up. "Sir! Sir!" he said. "Look, there's a racing car on that stamp, there."

"Yes," said Sir. "So what?"

"It's . . . um . . . the one in our model."

"No," said Darren. "Our model isn't a racing car at all. It's a high-speed post-office van . . . in Australia."

" 'Tisn't," said Mark. "It's a space-ship."

"Oh, heavens!" cried Sir, losing his cool. "Not again! But whatever it is, where is your writing? These are just pages of stamps. There's no writing at all."

"We'll bring it tomorrow," said Don.

They did bring some writing the next day, and it wasn't on stamps or racing cars. It was on boxing. That was what Mark's big brother had done his project on last term at the High School, and he let them copy it. But Sir couldn't prove it, could he?

6
Divided We Fall

Parents' Evening was quite near now, and the class began to get their work ready for display. Great care was taken of the racing car. Then Don had another idea.

"Could we take our car to show the infants?" he asked.

Sir was touched. Here were these tough boys, who were always fighting and making trouble, and now they wanted to give pleasure to the little children with the model they had worked so long on. They were human after all. How could Sir refuse?

"All right, then, but do take good care of it. We must have something to show that you've done some work this term."

Off they went, carrying their car between them. It left a large, paint-spattered, gap in the classroom. The room seemed bigger and quieter. We all settled down to the work of finishing our projects. It was so quiet that you could hear the clock ticking, the snip-snap of scissors, and the scraping sound of pencils being sharpened.

"Innit quiet, Sir," said Linda, in her sucking-up-to-Sir voice.

Sir looked happy for once. He smiled fondly at Linda. "Yes, love," he said, "so let's not spoil it, and get some good work done."

Get that, "love"? Sir must be in a really good mood.

There was a chance of getting a long playtime out of him, if all went well. We bent over our desks and scribbled away as though we meant it. But it was too good to last. There was a sound of distant shouting down the corridor, and it was coming nearer. We lifted our heads to listen.

"Get on with your work," said Sir, but nobody took any notice.

There were thumps and bangs mixed in with the shouting, then running boots. The door burst open, and Don fell into the room, carrying the front half of the racing car. He was crying and shouting at the same time, and Sir could make no sense of him. His nose was bleeding, and the blood and tears got mixed up and smeared all over his face and down his jumper. Sir sent Linda to get some wet paper-towels from the cloakroom to clean him up, and when she came back, she said,

"Oooh, Sir, there's a right mess in the infants' corridor" and Sir rushed out to see, and we crowded round Don to get a close look at the blood. All this excitement did something to Jimmy. He took out his new packet of coloured pencils, and began throwing them round the classroom. One hit Mumtaz in the face, and there was another fight going on by the time Sir came back with Darren and Mark, dragging the other half of the racing car behind them. When they saw Don they started laughing, and he went for them, and we cheered him on. It took Sir ages to stop all the fights, and get everyone sitting down again. It's a wonder the car wasn't smashed to bits, but there it still was, though in two halves, now.

When Don had wiped his face clean, and calmed down, Sir said, "Now, Donald, what was that all about, and who has broken your car? Since you've put a stop to the work of the whole class you'd better explain yourself."

"It was them," said Don, still snivelling.

Darren and Mark jumped up, with their fists ready.

"Now sit down," shouted Sir, "you can't solve problems by fighting. Let's just calm down and find out what happened. Never mind whose fault it was. What happened when you went out of that door?"

Don set out again on his story. Sir saw his mistake at once. I've told him thousands of times never ask Don to explain anything. Nobody had the foggiest what Don was on about. Sir asked Darren, but he'd wouldn't talk at all; he just screwed his face up and stared at Sir. Mark was no better. In the end, Sir just said they'd have to mend the car at dinner-time, and everyone could sit down quietly, now, and write their projects. We were all getting tired of the fuss, so we did sit down at our tables, our hands went up all over the room, with shouts of, "Sir, my pencil's gone!" and Sir said, "But you can't all have lost your pencils, all at once."

We had, though, every one of us. Except Jimmy. He had one pencil left, that he hadn't thrown away.

"I left mine on my desk, I know I did. It's not fair!" said Linda.

Mumtaz told Sir about Jimmy throwing his coloured pencils round the room, and we scrabbled on the floor to find them, and Sir said we could use them to write our projects, but the points kept breaking, and there was a queue at the pencil-sharpener till the bell went for

playtime, so nobody got any work done at all.

Our Timmy's a middle-infant, and when I saw him in the yard he told me all about what happened when they'd brought the car down to the infants. There was an argument between Don and Darren and Mark about which class to take the car to. Don wanted his little sister to play with it in Timmy's class, but Darren and Mark had brothers in the top infants, and wanted to take it there. They were stuck half way through the door, arguing about which way to go. Then a tug-of-war started, with Don trying to pull the car into the room, and Darren and Mark trying to pull it out. Miss Edwards came along, and then there was a snapping sound, and the car came apart.

Something fell out on to the floor with a sound of breaking plastic, and Rosie Sutcliffe said it was her missing cassette-player, and started to cry. Two cans of lager rolled out next, from the hidden drinks-box. Don tripped over the cans and lurched out into the corridor, and went for Darren and Mark. Miss Edwards got a good thump, trying to stop them, and went off to fetch Mrs. Foster. The fight moved down the corridor, and our Sir came out and stopped it when it got near enough, and the rest I knew.

I left Timmy to his skipping, and went to see what was going on in the junior-playground. You'd think there'd have been a big fight between Don and Mark about Darren. Not a bit of it! The three of them were good friends again, and they were passing sweets and crisps round in the bushes at the end of the school garden, planning their next move.

Sir had a new box of pencils when we went back in the classroom, so we had to do our work now. He didn't find out where all the pencils had been going till this lot disappeared as well, on the Thursday afternoon, when we had the road-safety film, and Sir made us all empty our trays, and spread them out on the tables. There were sixty-five pencils in Jimmy's tray!

"Where did you get these pencils, Jimmy?" said Sir, with murder in his voice.

Jimmy began to cry, but managed to blubber out, "Me mam got them from the shop," before Linda shouted, "That's mine! It's got my name on it! Look!" and we all crowded round, grabbing at our pencils.

Of course, Sir had to send for Mrs. Foster, and she took Jimmy off to her room. He stayed in for a whole week of playtimes, and his mother came in to complain, before he'd tell how he got the pencils. He'd been sneaking in at playtime, and going through all our trays, and getting our pencils. Mrs. Foster made him come and say he was sorry to the whole class. He wasn't sorry at all, you could tell that. He was laughing while he said it. Then Mrs. Foster said, "But why did you do it, Jimmy? You have plenty of pencils of your own."

Jimmy just hung his head and giggled. He didn't know why he did it. It was just the sort of thing that Jimmy does, and it's no use asking him why, he doesn't know himself. In the end, Mrs. Foster went away, and we got on with our work.

Don and his mates mended the car at dinner-time, and it looked just as good as before.

"At least we'll have something for Parents' Evening," said Sir.

You know, it amazes me. Teachers are always on about learning, and yet they never seem to learn.

7
Disaster!

"Bags I take the car home after Parents' Night," said Don.

"Bags you don't," said Darren.

"It's no good fighting about it again," said Mark, "it'll only get bust. Let's ask Sir to decide."

"Well done," said Sir. (He'd been listening in to all this). "I do think you're beginning to learn to do things with words instead of fists."

"Well, who can take it, then?" said Don.

"Let's toss up for it," said Sir in his cheerful voice. (First mistake; I saw it coming).

"It's not fair," said Don. "That car was my idea."

Sir took no notice. (Second mistake). He tossed the coin, Darren called and won. He tossed again, Darren against Mark, and Darren won again.

"It's a fiddle," muttered Don. Still Sir took no notice, and Don went mumbling and muttering back to his seat, and looking murder at Sir.

Everything would have been all right until Parents' Evening at least, if Mrs. Foster hadn't had one of her bright ideas. The car was rebuilt, and most of the projects were about finished when Sylvia Thompson came round on Monday morning with a note on a piece of paper.

Sir said, "All stop what you are doing, and listen carefully. Here's a message from Mrs. Foster. She says, 'I have seen such excellent work being done around the school, that I would like us all to share it before Parents' Evening on Wednesday. When your teacher tells you, please bring your work carefully to the Hall, and we will have a wonderful display for Tuesday's assembly. There will be ten minutes for each class to tell us about their work.' Did you all hear that?"

Jimmy made dalek-noises, and wandered round the classroom exterminating people. Sir took no notice. He was too worried by the message. He could spot trouble a mile off.

"We'd better have some good work to put in the Hall, so get on with it," said Sir.

Miraculously, for once, we all did. There was a knock at the door. It was Sylvia again.

"Mrs. Foster says could Donald and his group please bring their model car to the Hall, now."

"Now watch it, you lot," Sir growled, "we don't want any more trouble with that car."

They edged the car out of the door, and you could hear the class giving a little "oh" of relief at seeing them go. They had to cross the school garden to get to the Hall, and you could hear their voices fading into the distance, still talking about who should take the car home after Parents' Evening.

Jimmy was quietly sharpening his pencils, and he went on with this until they were all sharpened into stubs too short to use. But it kept him quiet, so Sir didn't interfere. The rest of us were writing away, and it was one of the peaceful times you remember for a long time. You could

hear the traffic on the flyover, and somebody walking along by the shops with a ghetto-blaster playing an old Beatles song. It was great. Real smooth. Then there was another sound added. You couldn't say when you first noticed it, or who first heard it, but, suddenly, everybody stopped what they were doing to strain their ears to listen. It was far away, and it echoed round the school like the sound-effects in a spooky horror-film. Whatever was it? Sir looked up to listen, then said, "Get on with your work. It's nothing to do with us."

The sounds came a bit nearer, and a bit clearer. There was mixed-up shouting and banging. Had somebody broken into Mrs. Gulam's room to nick the dinner-money? Had somebody kidnapped Mrs. Foster? No such luck. The sounds came still nearer. Sir got up to look out of the window. We all followed him. It was a battle. There were three muddy boys in the school garden, shouting and fighting. It had come on to rain, and they had landed up in the middle of a very wet flower-bed. They were rolling over and over in the mud, and one of them had just got his mouth full of it. They were so muddy that we didn't know at first who they were. Then we saw some broken blue boxes, and some pram-wheels scattered round. Mumtaz yelled, "It's Don and his mates! Look! Somebody's wrecked their car!"

"All sit down and get on with your work, at once," Sir

shouted, then ran out to stop the fight.

Of course, we all went straight back to the windows. We couldn't miss the fun, could we? It took ages for Sir to sort them out and stop the fight. Darren was crying and shouting at Sir, and Mark's nose was bleeding. Don's jeans were torn all down the leg, but he just sat in the mud looking fed up. Sir went off and brought Mrs. Foster and Mrs. Gulam, and they took the three of them off towards the Nursery. Nobody could guess why they went there, until Linda piped up. She helps with the little ones at dinner-time, and she knows a lot about the Nursery.

"I know," she said. "There's a shower in the Nursery! I bet they're going to put them in the shower!"

Naseem spotted Sir coming back, and we all ran to our desks and pretended to be working. He must have known we weren't really, but he didn't bother. He just sat down and went on with his marking. Later on, Sir sent me and Mumtaz and Linda to collect the bits of the racing car from the garden. There wasn't much left of it. We piled the bits in the car's place in the classroom. Sir was surprised to see quite a lot of things amongst the car's bits that had been missing from the classroom for a long time, but most of them were broken by now.

We didn't see Don, and Darren, and Mark for the rest of that morning. A kid from Class Three came for their PE things just before playtime, but they were kept in. Then we saw them getting their dinners. They looked red and clean, and their hair was spiky with the water. They were wearing old coats from the lost-property box. They had to sit at a table with Mrs. Foster for their dinner, and she

took them off to her room when they had finished. She
sent Linda to get their maths and writing books, and that
was that for the rest of the afternoon. We had a really
quiet time in the classroom, and Sir was so pleased with
us that he read us an extra chapter of "Mrs. Frisby and the
Rats of Nimh." Just before home-time, Imran was on
the way to the toilets when he spotted them getting into
Mrs. Foster's car. They were in real trouble this time. Mrs.
Foster would take them home and have a barney with
their parents.

I called for Mark after tea, but his mum said he wasn't
coming out, and banged the door hard.

That was the end of the model racing car, thank goodness. Don and his mates weren't allowed to play out for a week after that, and they had to stay in and do lines every single playtime and dinner-time. You couldn't get a word out of them about that last fight, or the car, or what happened when they went to the Nursery. They were never the same again.

On Parents' Evening, Don and his mates put their boxing-topic in the display, but their parents didn't come, anyway.

8
The School Trip

The summer term came round, and it was time to start planning the school trip. The rest of the school was going to Blackpool, but Sir said, "There's no need for us to go where everyone else goes. We can have a discussion, and make a democratic choice."

Alice's hand went up at once.

"What's demo . . . whatsit choice, Sir? Does it mean we're goin' to have a demo, like them students on the telly?"

"I'm glad you asked, Alice. No it's not like that. It means . . ."

Darren didn't let him finish.

"You talk about it for hours, then Sir tells you where you're going. I bet it'll be a boring museum."

Sir was upset. "Not at all, Darren. It's not a bit like that. We'll have a fair discussion, and listen to everyone's views, including yours, Darren, and then we'll have a vote on it."

Sir was getting annoyed now, and you could see that he really did want us to go to a museum, as Darren had said, but he wanted us to pick it for ourselves, after he'd brainwashed all the teachers' pets like Alice and Linda and mummy's boy Robbie. Then there was Jimmy. He'd go anywhere you told him. He'd jump off a cliff if you told him to. I was getting worried that it would be a museum in the end, till Don woke up from his dreams of fish-and-chips, and said, "I want to go to the safari-park. Me uncle took me there last Easter, and it was great. There was this tiger, and . . ."

"All right, Don, all right." Sir could see that Don was taking over, and he'd have to get a word in quick. "There are many other possibilities . . ."

Now Darren joined in, "Don't mess about, Sir, we all want to go to the safari-park, don't we?"

Mumbled shouts of, "Yerss, we do," and, "right on, Darren!" came from the back of the class. Then Linda piped up. She made her big-eyes, baby-doll, look at Sir, and said, "It would be nice, Sir, at the safari-park, and I've never been."

That finished Sir, never mind the democracy bit. He couldn't resist Linda when she put her act on. I could see he'd given in. He went on with putting a list of suggestions on the board, including Jimmy's idea of a trip in the Space Shuttle, and having a vote on it, but Linda and Don between them had settled it. One half of the class knew that Don would bash them if they didn't vote for the safari-park, and most of the other half were in Linda's secret club. So that was it. Sir chalked the votes on the board, not forgetting his own, to be fair.

MUSEUM 1
SPACE SHUTTLE 1
SAFARI PARK 29

Jimmy burst into tears and rolled on the floor in despair

when he saw his chance of a ride in the Space Shuttle fading, and no one could stop him or cheer him up. Alice had to take him to Mrs. Foster in the end, and she gave him a toffee out of her tin.

The next thing was to collect the money, and book the coach, and pick a date. You might have known there'd be a catch in it. Sir said it would be a good piece of practical maths for us, and we all had to work how much it would be for each one, when we'd added up the prices of the coach and the admission to the safari-park. Not one person in the class could divide by thirty-one, but Don did it on the computer while Sir was talking to Mrs. Peckham about a broken milk-bottle, and Sir was ever so pleased when he came back and found that we all had the right answer. Then he asked to see our working-out, and nobody had any, not even Jimmy, so he knew it was a trick, then, and he made us stay in at playtime to do it properly.

"It's not worth going to the rotten old safari-park, if we have to do this rotten dividing," grumbled Don.

There was a mumble of revolt all round the class. This made Sir get stroppy, and he started on; "The trip's really meant to be educational, you know. We could do a project about the animals, when we get back. We could take our clip-boards and draw them, and make notes."

Oh, that did it! Not even Linda and Robbie were standing for that. Linda's hand jabbed at the ceiling, and she told Sir straight. "I'm not bringing my money if it's going to be work, so there! I've had to save my spends, and I've had no sweets for two weeks and . . ."

"All right, Linda, all right, it was only a suggestion."

He tried to shush her up, but she went on ever so long. She has a real temper when she gets going, and she's not a bit scared of Sir when she's like that.

Sir had to give in, and promise there'd be no more work about the safari-park. But you have to watch these teachers, you know. Mind you, it didn't stop him sneaking things in about animals during the weeks before the big day came. All the poems and stories he read us mysteriously turned out to be about tigers and kangaroos, and things like that, and the only way he could get us to listen properly was by reading "Apple tart makes you fart" every now and then. We got him to go on with "Mrs. Frisby and the Rats of Nimh", though.

"Well, it is about animals, Sir," said Robbie.

"Rats, Robbie, rats," said Sir, with his smarmy smile. "They don't have rats at the safari-park."

"Bet they do," said Don. "I saw some at Chester zoo. In a cage. Desert rats. Great!"

Sir nearly got us into a topic about Africa, a week later. But Jimmy came in useful for once. He's always getting books from the library, and he had a big book about animals. It said that many of the big animals come from Africa, and you may be lucky enough to see them in this country in a safari-park. Linda and Alice were in there in a flash; "Oooh, Sir, you promised. No more work about the trip."

So he had to drop it, specially as only about half of us had brought the money, and Sir had already paid for the coach.

Then he tried a topic on transport, but Naseem said,

49

"Oh, but, Sir, we'll be going to the safari-park in a coach, and that's transport, and you did promise, Sir."

"Well, there must be something we can do!" moaned Sir. "We can't just sit around doing nothing till trip-day comes."

"Why not, Sir!" we all said, but he didn't think it was funny.

In desperation, Sir said we could do a project about babies. We didn't want to do that at first, but Darren got everybody together at playtime, and said it would be a good chance to ask Sir where babies come from, so we said we'd do that project. Then Jimmy got a book about babies out of the library, and it had a picture in it of a man and a woman with nothing on, so we had a good laugh in the end.

9
Lion-Bars

It seemed as though the day of the trip would never come, but it did come round at last, as things usually do. We were going on the Thursday, and on the Monday morning we had a discussion about whose parents would be coming with us, and how much money we could take, and how many bags of crisps and cans of drink we were allowed. Sir got difficult again. He pricked his ears up at the mention of cans of drink.

"I really do think we will have to ban cans of fizzy drink," he said, rather sniffily. "I haven't forgotten last year. There were two twits who flooded the coach with their cans. They shook them up to make them fizz, and they squirted out like fire-hoses. I've never seen such a mess. JOLLY-WAY COACHES have refused to give us any more bookings ever since, and they are the cheapest firm for miles."

"But, Sir, that's not fair, that was last year's class," said Linda. "You can't blame us for that." She gave Sir one of her Paddington Stares.

"I'm not blaming you, Linda; I just don't want it happening again, that's all. I'm quite sure none of you would do anything like that."

"Har, har, har," came from the back of the class; Don had wakened up.

"And don't get any silly ideas," said Sir. "We can easily send you home if you don't behave yourself properly, when we get there."

"You can't send me home, 'cos me mam's coming on the trip," said Don, grinning his oiliest grin.

"All the more reason to behave yourself, then," said Sir, but he knew he'd lost that one.

"Sir, can we take cans if we promise not to make a mess with them?" said Linda.

"For the last time," said Sir, loudly, "NO CANS."

"What about crisps, then?" said Darren.

"Not more than two bags each," said Sir. "We don't

want you being sick on the coach."

"Oh, Sir!" The shouts of protest went up all over the class. Our class are devils for crisps. Besides, we knew that Don had nicked a box from his dad's shop, and he was planning to sell them at half-price for the trip. He looked very put out at this remark.

"Waaaaaaaaaaaaaaaaaaa!"

"What in heaven's name . . .?" said Sir.

It was Jimmy. He had banged his head down on his table, and begun to wail like a ghost-train.

"What wrong with that boy, now?" said Sir.

"I know, Sir," said Mumtaz. "He's already bought his drinks and his crisps for the trip. He's had them packed up since last Saturday, and he has four cans of Cola, and a multipak of crisps – two of vinegar, two beef, and two cheese-and-onion."

"Good grief," said Alice.

"All right, Jimmy, you can take your drinks and crisps," said Sir. "Anything for peace."

In a flash, a dozen hands went up, and everybody started shouting, "Sir! Sir! Can I take mine! I'll cry if you don't let me. Waaaaa! Waaaa!"

Sir had had enough. He stood up and shouted, "SHUT UP! EVERYBODY! Now listen. Stop that silly noise, Jimmy. OK, it's the same rule for everybody, as I said before; no cans, and not more than two bags of crisps, including you, Jimmy."

Of course, that started Jimmy off again. Alice had to take him off to Mrs. Foster, as usual, because nobody could hear anything until he'd gone.

Then we had to decide whose mums and dads were coming with us, and Jimmy got left out of that with being out of the room, so there were ructions when he came back, because he wanted his mum to come, and all the seats had been filled.

"One more thing," said Sir, at home-time. "This is very important. You must do as you're told on the trip, and you must not wander off on your own. A safari-park can be a dangerous place, and we don't want anyone getting eaten by a lion, do we?"

"Yes, Sir!" shouted everybody, pointing at Jimmy. Poor kid, I felt sorry for him just then, even if he is a pain in the neck; it was a bit mean to say that. But he wasn't bothered. He just laughed. He seemed to think the idea funny, him being eaten by a lion.

"I'll give it a Lion-Bar," he said, with his daft smile all over his face. He would, too. He had me dead worried, I

don't know about Sir. I could just see that kid climbing into the lions' den to give them a Lion-Bar each; you could see the idea blossoming in what Jimmy had instead of a brain.

When everybody had stopped laughing, Sir said, "It's no joke. Not funny at all. There have been cases of children being mauled by lions, and I don't want anything to spoil our trip, so please remember what I have said."

"What about teachers, Sir," said Mark. "Have any teachers been eaten by lions?"

"I don't know, but some nasty little boys may have been *thrown* to the lions," said Sir, "and it could happen again."

Then the bell went, and it was time to go home. Jimmy's mother always came for him, and I heard him talking to her in the cloakroom.

"... and Sir says if there are any nasty little boys in our class, he's going to throw them to the lions for their dinner."

"He said *what?*" said Jimmy's mum. She always took

everything dead seriously, like her kid. The last I saw of her, she was stamping along the corridor to the staff-room, to see Sir. I bet she chewed his ear off!

10
On the Way

It was a lovely day on Thursday. The rest of the school was going off to Blackpool, but we were being different; we were going to the Safari Park. How excited we were. If only school were like this every day! And what a sight we were, coming down the road, loaded up with our bags of sandwiches! You'd think we were going away for months, looking at the food some of us had brought. We kept our cans of drink well out of sight, in case Sir saw them.

Jimmy had about ten bags of crisps, and four cans of drink, but his mum said she was coming with us, so Sir couldn't say anything about it, could he? Don was wearing one of these hats you see these hunters wearing on films; he must have borrowed it from one of his uncles; and he had a rifle over his shoulder. When Sir saw it he nearly blew up!

"Where do you think you're going? And what is that? A gun? You must be mad, boy. We're not going on safari; we're going to a safari-*park*, which is totally different. You can leave that lot in Mrs. Foster's room for the day."

Don started on one of his explanations, but Sir just had to stop him, as we would never have left at all if he hadn't. He shunted him off to Mrs. Foster with the hat and the gun, and got on with the register. Jimmy suddenly started leaping around and yelping like a puppy. Sir was just starting to shout at him to shut up and sit down, when Jimmy's mum walked in and stopped Sir in his tracks.

"Oh, er, good morning, Mrs. Marley, can I . . .?"

"I'll have to come wiv yer," said Mrs. Marley.

"Oh, but, Mrs. Marley, we've filled . . ."

"That's all right, they can squash up to make room."

"I'm afraid the coach company won't allow . . ."

"I'm coming," said Mrs. Marley, glaring at Sir.

"Well, er, hum . . ." Sir didn't know what to say. In the end, all he did say was, "Oh, well, I suppose it'll be all right. Perhaps they'll not notice."

Then Don's dad came in, with the gun and helmet in his hands, and started on at Sir. "I've just seen my lad going to the Head's room with these. I don't know what fool told

him to do that; he's taking them with him, in't he? He can't go without his uncle's hat and gun. He's been looking forward to it!"

This was when I began to feel sorry for Sir, and, besides, I thought we might never get there at this rate, so I put my hand up and said, 'They'll not let you in with a gun. My uncle took one, and they wouldn't let him in. Honest."

In the end, Don left the gun and took the hat, muttering that he'd get Sir for that, you see if he wouldn't. Jimmy was still yelping and twitching, and Sir said to Mrs. Marley, "Is your son . . . er . . . all right?"

"All right? Course he's all right. He's only excited. He's seen the coaches, hasn't he? It's natural for a child to be excited."

Excited! He was just about paralytic, and Mrs. Marley, too, began to twitch in tune with her Jimmy. Then the other parents arrived, and the coach-drivers began hooting their horns, and it was time to go.

When Jimmy got outside, he saw the little kids going off to Blackpool with their buckets and spades and their swimming things, and decided he'd rather go with them. His mum held on to him, and he kicked and screamed and cried his eyes out. She held on to him, and gave him a good bat round the legs, and more or less stuffed him into the coach. Then there was a fuss because she wasn't supposed to be on the coach at all, and there was no seat for her, and she hadn't paid. Then it turned out that the driver's cousin's sister was Mrs. Marley's sister's sister-in-law, or something like that, and the driver said, "Rules is made to be bent, if not broken, eh?" and gave Mrs. Marley and Jimmy the best seat at the front.

The little kids had opened the windows on their coaches, and they were shouting across at us, "Yah! Stupid! Going to the rotten safari-park! We're going to Blackpool, and we're going in the sea."

They knew we couldn't get to them, so they could say what they liked. They never seemed to think that we'd get them on the way home from school after the trip. Our lot shouted back, until Sir made us all sit down. He gave us another jawing about behaving ourselves, and we were off.

Nothing much happened on the way. Jimmy was sick twice, with sitting at the front and drinking fizzy drinks. Don and Darren had a fight at the back, and we had to stop whilst six boys went behind a wall in the country for a pee. You should have seen the girls trying to look! We all had a good laugh when a cow came up behind them, and

Naseem shouted, "Look out, there's a bull!" and they all had a fright, and had to run for it before they'd finished. Mark wet himself all down his leg, and Jimmy forgot to fasten his fly, and got another smacking from his mum. I think he was sorry already that he'd asked her to come on the trip, and everybody felt a bit sorry for him. He even asked if he could go and sit with Sir, but his mum wouldn't let him.

We sang a few songs, and Sir stopped us singing the rude ones we sing when there are no parents with us, and then we were there.

11
The Safari Park

When we arrived at the Safari Park there was a long line of coaches waiting to go in, and we had to wait our turn in the baking-hot sunshine. We had all the windows open, but it was still bloomin' hot.

"Can we get out for a walk, Sir?" came from the back.

"Who was that?" said Sir, standing up at the front. "Darren? No, Darren, you can't get out for a walk."

"Oh, Sir, it's hot in here."

There were moans and cries from all over the coach.

"We'll soon be going in to see all the animals, and then we'll go to the picnic area, and you'll get cool under the trees. And there's a super adventure playground, too. Just be patient for a while."

Then Mark had a bright idea. "Please, Sir, can I go to the toilet?"

"No, you can't; not till we get to the picnic area."

"But, Sir, I can't wait!"

This was a tough one for Sir. We all remembered that Mark had already wet himself. Then Jimmy's hand went up, and he began to wriggle in his seat.

"I want to go! I want to go!" he yelled.

With Jimmy's mum sitting there, all Sir could do was grit his teeth, force a smile, and say, 'Now, Jimmy, you did go behind the wall, surely you don't want to go again, already?"

Jimmy's mum chipped in. "Mr. Jackson – the child says he wants to go, so he wants to go. He doesn't tell lies, doesn't my Jimmy. There must be a lavvy somewhere round here, surely!"

Now more and more hands went up, and waved about urgently trying to catch Sir's eye.

"Well . . . er . . . I don't know . . ." said Sir. "I'll ask the driver."

There were more mutterings up at the front, then Sir said, "For the ones who really and truly want to go to the toilet, and can't wait, Mrs. Marley will take the girls, and Mr. Robinson will take the boys. I'm told there is a toilet near the entrance to the park, and you should have time if you get a move on. But don't blame me if you miss seeing the animals because you'd rather spend the day in the toilets."

Quite a few hands went down after Sir said that, but all the same, there were six or seven kids in each group that got out of the coach and went off ahead along the road to the toilets. Don was one of them, and he gave me a two-finger sign as he went. He thought I was a twit to stay put in the hot bus, but I didn't want to go to the loo, any more than he did, as we'd both been behind the wall, and I didn't mean to risk missing the animals when we'd come all that way and saved our spends for weeks and weeks to come. So off he went, complete with his African hunter's hat.

As soon as the toilet groups had got out of sight, the line of coaches began to move. There was no way that our

driver could wait, as there was no space at the side of the road to park, and we couldn't stop the whole queue. Robbie White's mum was looking very worried.

"Don't worry," said Sir, "they're sure to catch up with us at the entrance, where the toilets are. There are dozens of coaches in front of us."

But there was a man standing in the road, signalling our part of the queue of coaches to turn off down a side road. Our driver leaned out of his window to ask him what was going on.

"We've opened another entrance, to clear the queue," he shouted.

"But some of our children have gone the other way, to the toilets," yelled Sir from the open door.

"Can't help that," said the man. "The notice tells you to stay with your coach. I expect you'll see them at the picnic site. We can't take responsibility. Now please get a move on, you're holding up the whole queue."

The coach moved off, picking up speed, down the side road.

"My god!" said Sir, putting his head in his hands. "Now we've lost two parents and...let's see..." (He stopped to count us for the umpteenth time).

"Yes...sixteen children and two parents."

Mrs. White looked as though she was going to jump off the moving coach to go in search for her dear little Robbie. He's the softest little mummy's darling in our school, and a lion would have to be starving to eat him. Any decent lion would spit him out in disgust.

Anyway, there was Mrs. White trying to get to the door, and Sir holding her back, and trying to get her to sit down again.

"I'm quite sure they'll be all right," said Sir, not looking at all sure. "They have Mr. Robinson and Mrs. Marley to look after them, and they are both very responsible people."

You could have fooled me. If Mr. Robinson's anything like Don, he'll have shot an elephant by now, and be selling its tusks down on the main road. As for Mrs. Marley and her Jimmy! Enough said. Mrs. White sat down, looking pale and shaky, and glared at Sir as though he had done it all on purpose.

We soon arrived at our entrance to the Safari Park. There was no sign of the toilet-parties at all. Sir asked about them, and the man selling the tickets said, "I shouldn't worry, Sir. They'll be sure to meet up with you at the picnic site. All the coaches stop there when they

come out. I expect they'll be taken through on someone else's coach. They'll be OK. And do see that all your windows are closed, won't you. Our monkeys are even worse than some of yours!"

He laughed at this, but Sir said, "Don't say that till you know this lot better," and he didn't laugh at all.

When we had closed all the coach windows, it was

hotter and stuffier than ever, but we were soon under the trees in the park, and in the shade. We all crowded to the windows, and looked out, hoping to see lions and tigers and elephants, but all I could see was trees and grass and a few pigeons.

"It's bloomin' hot in here," Mumtaz whispered. "I'm going to open a window. I'm melting"

"Better not," I said. "You'll get done. Sure to, if Sir sees you."

But he opened it just the same.

12
The Hunter

"Why do we have to keep all the windows shut, anyway?" grumbled Mumtaz. "I don't see why. It's far too hot. It's just a silly rule, like all these stupid rules we have at school. *Do this. Do that. Don't do that, that, and that,* a thousand million trillion times over every day."

"It's not as bad as that," I said.

"Oh, isn't it just?" he said, punching me in the stomach. (But not hard enough to start a fight).

"Anyway," I said, "there's a good reason for this rule. It's because of safety. They've got all these dangerous animals here haven't they? They'd look silly if kids got eaten by lions, and they'd soon be out of business. A few gory pics in The Mirror and they'd be closed down in a flash."

"*Lions?*" said Mumtaz. "Lions, getting through that little window? Don't be stupid! Nothing bigger than a sparrow could get through there."

Linda was listening from the seat in front, and now she pushed her face between the head-rests, to join in. "What about snakes?" she said, screwing up her face in an URRRRGHHHH look. "They could get through. Easy. And if it was a poisonous one, it would bite you, and then you'd die in horrible agony, and serve you right."

"It might just as well bite you," I said. "And I should

think it will, when it sees that silly hat."

"Well I hope it gets you first," she said, "and uses all its poison up on you, then I'll be OK. And it's not a silly hat, it's my holiday hat from the camp. Anyway, I'm telling Sir if you don't shut that window."

She was just going to put her hand up to tell, when the bus stopped, and the Safari Park man began telling us about where we were.

"This is the area where we keep most of our monkeys and apes," he said. "You will see some in the picnic-area, but those are quite harmless. Some of the ones here can be vicious, and that's why you cannot get out of the coach to see them, or open any windows."

There was a series of thumps on the roof of the coach.

"There; did you hear that?" said the man. "That's a group of macacques jumping on the roof. I hope, driver, that there are no loose fittings on this coach?"

There was a twang and a ripping sound as a large monkey began tearing the radio-aerial off. The driver started to swear at the Safari Park man, and went red in the face.

"Look!" said Mumtaz. "Look at that lot!"

The monkeys were swarming all over the coach now. They were pulling at every bit of shiny chrome trim, to see if it was loose, and peering in at us, showing their long yellow teeth, and thumping and biting at the bodywork of the coach. One of them peed all down the window; a bright yellow stream that just about sent all of us into screaming hysterics.

"Look!" yelled Darren. "Look at its thing!"

"Shut up," said Linda, "don't be rude."

Linda had turned to the front, so she didn't see the long hairy arm that came through the window. I was just saying to Mumtaz, "You'd better shut that window, mate," but I was too late. The monkey was too quick for us. It grabbed at Linda's hat, and got hold of a bunch of hair as well.

"Stop it, you stupid boys!" shouted Linda. "I know it's you! Oh! Ouch! Stop it! Please, stop it, you're hurting. Sir! Sir!"

I tried to pull the monkey's arm away, but it felt as hard as iron. It gave a last tug, and pulled Linda's hat through the window, along with quite a bit of her hair. You should have heard her scream! Well, you couldn't blame her. But by the time she'd twisted round in her seat, the monkey had gone, and she still thought it was us that had pulled her hair and thrown her hat out of the window. She went for us, biting and scratching for all she was worth. She was worse than the monkey! Sir came striding up the coach to pull us apart, yelling at us as he came. "Stop that fighting at once! This is the last time you come on a trip with me!" and all the other things that teachers shout when they get properly upset. Then we all saw the monkey, sitting on the bonnet of the coach, trying to eat Linda's hat. Sir's eye went from the monkey, to Linda, to us, to the open window. You could see him working it all out. We were going to get done one way or the other, that was for sure. But something else happened at that moment that made Sir forget all about our little battle.

"What on earth is *that*?" he said, in a ghastly voice, pointing to a gap between the trees. It looked like a hunter's hat. An *African* hunter's hat; poking up behind some low bushes, and creeping along from one hiding place to another.

"I've seen that hat somewhere before," said Sir. "Or one very much like it."

You could tell he didn't want to believe what he could see. He had the look he has when Don shows him a page of his writing, and the mess makes him feel sick.

There was shouting somewhere on the other side of the coach, and the person in the hat began to run. He came out from the bushes. It was Don! And he had a gun!

"My god, what is that boy doing?" yelled Sir. "He'll get himself killed!"

Sir ran back to the front of the coach, and began

shouting at the Safari Park man. The man shouted back, and the driver joined in, all going on about different things.

A lot of things happened very quickly now. Outside, a gang of monkeys began to close in on Don, showing their teeth, and looking very nasty. He was fumbling with the old gun, but he didn't seem to be able to do anything with it. In the end he began to swing it round like a club, to keep the monkeys back. This worked for a time, but you could see that some of them were getting up into the trees, ready to drop on him from above.

Inside the coach, Sir was trying to open the door, and the Safari Park man was struggling to stop him. I suppose Sir had some idea of going to rescue Don, heaven knows why, and the man was stopping him, because, once the door was open, we'd have the coach full of those awful monkeys! The driver was revving his engine, and pressing hard on the horn-button, because he wanted to get his precious coach away before the monkeys dismantled it completely, but there were two coaches blocking the road in front of us, taking not a blind bit of notice of all this commotion. In the end, Sir did get out, and he went sprinting across the grass towards Don. The monkeys, amazed at this new sight, ran a short distance, then began to pelt Sir and Don with sticks and bits of bark, and small stones. Then they began to close in again, whilst Don and Sir huddled together against a tree. More and more monkeys were coming, now, to see what the noise was about, and to join in. There were thousands of them!

I don't know what would have happened if the park's rescue-truck hadn't come, just in time, with its sirens screaming and its lights flashing. I think they would have torn them to tiny pieces. Just think! We could have got rid of two nuisances in one go! No, that's not fair, is it? But, anyway, they did get rescued, so that was all right. You could see that their clothes were in a right old mess, and they were bleeding a bit where the sticks had hit them, and Don looked as though he'd had a nasty bite on his leg. The rescue-team whipped them off to the first-aid station, so we didn't get a close look. A pity, that.

That left Mrs. White and Mr. Khan in charge of us, as the surviving parents, and a fat lot of use they were. Mrs. White was just about convinced that her Robbie had been eaten by lions, so she was reduced to a nervous jelly, and Mr. Khan was talking at great speed in Pakistani; even Mumtaz couldn't understand him, because it was a different brand of Pakistani from the one Mumtaz knows. Whatever he was saying, he was very upset about something. It was a lucky thing that the Safari Park man had stayed with us.

He soon calmed us down and took over. It was a one-way system through the park, so we simply went on with the normal tour, with every single window tightly closed now. We saw the lions; they were in the next enclosure, and couldn't have got at Don at all. They looked very sleepy in the sunshine, but nobody offered when the man said, "Anyone fancy getting out to play with them?"

Then we saw the tigers, and the elephants, and the camels, and deer, and all the other animals. It was great!

13
Home Again!

When we had finished seeing all the animals, the coach drove into the car-park, and the Safari Park man said, "The toilets are over there, and I'm sure you'll all be ready to spend a penny by now." (We were!) "It's quite safe to walk about in this part of the park, but watch out for the small monkeys who live in the trees. They're a real pack of thieves. Your teacher will be in the first-aid post over there, so come back to the coach when you've been to the toilets, and I'll send him over to you."

We dashed off for a pee, and what a laugh we had! There were some seats not far away, and there they were, all that stupid lot we had lost at the beginning, when they'd gone off to the toilets, sitting in a row, with Mrs. Marley, looking real fed up. They might not have been eaten by the lions, but they looked as though they'd have enjoyed that more than sitting outside the toilets waiting for us.

Mrs. Marley was furious. She was blazing mad. "Where's that ruddy teacher of yours?" she shouted. "We've been sat here for hours waiting for you lot. Where did you get to? We didn't dare move in case we missed you, and then you never came. And this lot have been fighting, and crying, and god knows what. And Don Robinson's wandered off heaven knows where to, with that blooming hat and his dad's gun, and his dad's gone off to look for him. For all we know the lions have got him. Where is that idiotic teacher? And when are we going to see these animals?"

We fell about laughing, and that made her worse. I thought she was going to have a fit. Then Linda piped up, "Please, Mrs. Marley, Sir's in the first-aid with Don Robinson, and we've seen the animals, and they were great."

"In the first-aid? With Don Robinson? How did he get there? Did you say you've *seen* the animals? Do you mean you've been enjoying yourselves while we've been sat here waiting for you?"

That was it. She did have a fit. She simply couldn't speak. Her eyes bulged, and she kept saying, "*What?*" and working her mouth about. Her Jimmy slumped off the seat, and rolled about on the grass, crying. His mum looked as though she'd like to join him. I felt sure she'd murder Sir when he came out of the first-aid place.

We all went back to the coach, and Mrs. Marley started on at the coach-driver about going through the safari park again so that the others could see the animals. That started him off, then. He swore at Mrs. Marley, and then, when he'd calmed down a bit, he said, "No way am I going through there again with my coach. NEVER! Just look at it! Look what them ruddy monkeys have done to my paint-work and my chrome! I'll be claiming for that. You'll see!"

By the time Sir and Don came out of the first-aid place, with their bandages and plasters on, looking like survivors

from a war, Mrs. Marley was getting tired, so she didn't murder Sir, she just shouted at him for about half an hour. I thought that was a bit unfair, as Sir had told them at the beginning that they might be spending the day at the toilets if they went off when they did. And it wasn't his fault, was it?

Then Mr. Robinson came back and found his long lost kid, and wanted to know how he came to be all bandaged up.

"Has that child been mauled by lions?" he wanted to know.

Sir told his part of the story, but Don wouldn't say a word about how he'd got amongst the big baboons.

"It's a wonder anybody noticed the difference," said Jimmy, and got a clip on the ear from his mum.

We had one more good laugh that day.

Sir said he would ask the driver to stop on the way home at some place where you could go for a ride on a boat, up a river. We'd all go for a boat trip, and Sir would pay for it out of School Fund, and that would make up for everything going wrong at the Safari Park.

"Great!" said Mumtaz. "A free ride on a boat as well! What a day!"

The boat was great. It had a little bar on it, and Sir bought drinks for all the parents. Then he bought ice-creams for us kids, and Mrs. Marley had an ice-cream as well, as she was specially upset, and needed buttering up as much as possible before we got back and she could make a complaint to Mrs. Foster. I've never known Sir be so nice to anybody. Creep!

A crowd of gulls kept swooping round the boat, and people were holding bread up for them. They whizzed down and grabbed it without stopping.

It was a lovely ride up the river, but the others still said it wasn't fair, as we'd been round the Safari Park as well. We just said, "Yah! to you."

Everything seemed very quiet and peaceful, and all at once I noticed why. It was because Mrs. Marley had stopped yakking on. She had gone very quiet, and she was leaning over the rail of the boat looking down at the water.

"Is she going to jump?" I whispered to Mumtaz.

"I think she's going to be sick," he said.

The boat was pitching about a bit, and ice-cream on top of a double gin-and-tonic hadn't been a good idea at all. Oooh, she did look green!

"Watch your teeth, mum," said Jimmy, as she leaned further over to be sick into the river. Just in time, she snatched out her false-teeth and held them clear as she let fly with a fountain of sick. Urgh! Nasty! There was a large gull perched on the mast, and when it saw the teeth held up it must have thought that here was a tasty piece of bread being offered to it. It made a loud sqwawk,

swooped down, snatched Mrs. Marley's teeth in its big yellow beak, and flew out across the water. When it saw what it had got, it dropped the teeth and flew away in disgust, and we saw them splash down into the water.

Spitting out the last of the sick, Mrs. Marley moaned, "My teef! My teef! I've loft my teef!"

The whole lot of us were holding on to each other, laughing our heads off. Poor Mrs. Marley! I did feel sorry for her, but I just couldn't stop laughing. Even Sir had a hard job to keep his face straight.

We laughed and sang all the way home. Mumtaz and me, we said it was the best school-trip ever. But some people didn't agree at all. As for Sir, he said it would be the museum next year, and there would be no voting on it.

14
Christmas is Coming!

The Pakistani kids are lucky because they have two Christmasses. They have one of their own, called Divali, and then they have our Christmas. Well, we were lucky this year because we all had Divali. We made a play about it in the Hall. I was the leader of an army of monkeys. I liked that. There was a prince and a beautiful princess in it, and a magic arrow. We all made some special lamps, with oil in them. And then we had a lot of candles, and we had a procession into the Hall, in the dark, with everybody carrying a candle. It was lovely. It was like a dream, specially when Sir lit some sticks of stuff that smoked and made a nice smell.

Mumtaz, and Naseem, and Dipali, and Waseem, all had a day off school, as well, for Divali. Linda put her hand up, and said, "Sir, it's not fair. We should have a day off too."

But Sir only said, "Just think how lucky you are, getting all these extra lessons, and for no extra charge."

And Linda said, "That's not funny, Sir!"

I still haven't told you how Linda lost her knickers, or about the time Sir's trousers were on fire, but I'm coming to it, I promise. All sorts of crazy things happen in our school when Christmas is getting near. I don't know whether the kids or the teachers are the worst. And I don't know if anybody else has teachers like ours. Some of them are really weird.

Every year, we have a school concert at Christmas, when each class has to put on some kind of act. Well, lots of schools do that, I suppose. But our school has an extra.

The teachers put on a pantomime for the kids to watch. I think our Sir must organise it, because he's forever nipping out of the classroom and leaving us to get on with it on our own, and sending notices round about staff meetings. But all the teachers pretend that they're not doing it at all! If you ask about it, Sir just says, "What pantomime? I don't know anything about a pantomime."

And then, when it happens, they pretend that it was a real giant, and a real princess, and everything, that visited the school to tell us their story. See what I mean about being weird? The little kids, the ones in the Nursery, they swallow the whole thing, some of them anyway. When our Timmy was four he cried his eyes out at Christmas, because he thought his teacher had been eaten by a dragon. It was no good telling him that Sir had made the dragon with paper, and string, and a bunch of garden-canes, and a load of powder-paint. Mum had to carry Timmy round to the staff-room to show him that Mrs. Bell was alive and well, but he still didn't believe us, not properly, anyway.

To give the teachers time to practise their pantomime, Mrs. Foster used to show us films in the hall. They were really boring films, and I fell asleep one year in the middle of the film, so Mrs. Foster sent me to stand in the corridor with my hands on my head.

I got bored with standing in the corridor, so I put my

hands in my pockets and had a quiet walk round the
school. Mrs. Foster was too busy with the film to notice
what I was up to, and I thought I might find out what this
year's pantomime was going to be. I did, and I had a good
laugh as well. There they all were, practising in the hall,
with Sir telling them what to do. It looked as though Mrs.
Bell was safe from dragons this year, as she seemed to be
The Sleeping Beauty, lying on her bed.

I had a good view, as I hid myself behind some thick

curtains that hang right down to the floor. I was nearly spotted, because somebody's mum called to see Mrs. Bell, and Sir came out of the hall to talk to her, and almost stepped on my foot as he passed.

I could see Sir and the mum through a slit in this curtain, and I nearly died with trying not to laugh. There was Sir, wearing a pair of goblin's ears, and with make-up on his face, talking to this mum about getting her little girl into the Nursery next term. And the mum didn't bat an eyelid! You'd think she met goblins every day. I heard her say, "Could I just have a word with Mrs. Bell?"

And Sir said, "Well, no, I'm sorry, but you can't just now. She's asleep in the Hall."

The mum still didn't bat an eyelid. She said, "Will she be long?"

And Sir said, (honest, he did say this,) "She'll be about a hundred years."

"It's all right," said the mum, "I'm not in a hurry. I'll wait."

I didn't hear any more, because I was laughing so much that I was wetting myself. And suddenly I knew that I couldn't wait one second. I just had to make a dash for it to the toilets. Of course Sir spotted me, and shouted, "Hey! You! Stop!"

But I couldn't stop. I would have been in worse trouble if I had done. So I kept going. But I knew he'd be waiting for me when I came out of the loo. The trouble was, he still had his goblin-ears on, and I had a bad time keeping my face straight, even though I was getting done. So, there we were, him with his goblin make-up, and me with a wet leg,

and it went something like this.

"What exactly were you up to behind that curtain?"

"Er . . . nothing, Sir."

"What do you mean, nothing? You couldn't be doing nothing! You wouldn't wrap yourself up in a curtain to do nothing, idiot!"

"No, sir."

"Well, then, what *were* you doing?"

"Watching, Sir."

"Watching what?"

"The pantomime, Sir."

"What pantomime?"

"Your pantomime, Sir. With the other teachers."

"Nonsense. There's no pantomime. That was a staff meeting . . . What was it?"

"A staff meeting, Sir."

"Good. And if you tell anyone, anyone at all, that a staff meeting is a pantomime, then you'll be doing lines all afternoon on Friday, when everyone else is in the Hall, enjoying a staff meeting. Understand?"

"Yes, Sir."

"And as it's Christmas I'll let you off the punishment you deserve for hiding behind that curtain instead of being wherever you should be."

"Thanks, Sir."

"And as you know about the staff meeting, you might as well come and help with some scene-shifting."

"Thanks, Sir."

"And we'll see how good you are at keeping a secret."

"*Yes*, Sir!"

You see, now, what I mean when I say our teachers are weird. But Sir is a good sport sometimes.

I had a great time, helping with that pantomime, I mean that staff-meeing, and you won't believe this, but I did keep the secret. Until now.

15
The Fairy on the Christmas Tree

There was no time at all for lessons now. What with making decorations and practising for the concert; choir and carol practices; getting ready for Christmas parties; and collecting for Oxfam; there was no time for messing

about with maths and English, and all our exercise books were safely stashed away in Sir's cupboard until it was all over. Don and his mates looked a lot happier now that they had forgotten that such things as writing and sums existed. There were times when they semed almost human. Don was even seen picking the little kids up when they fell on the ice in the yard at playtime, and Darren went to read stories in the Nursery.

One of Sir's special Christmas jobs was putting the tree up in the Hall. You see, he was Deputy Head, and Deputy Heads always do that. Mrs. Foster, our headmistress, always went bonkers about this, because she wanted to do it herself, and she always shouted at Sir for doing it wrong. She'd walk all round it, squinting at it, then say it wasn't straight. Then Sir had to go up a wobbly ladder to straighten it, and she said it still wasn't straight. This would go on for hours, and we had to sit at the back of the Hall with our boring reading books, till Don and Darren started a fight, and Sir took us back to the classroom, leaving Mrs. Foster fiddling with the tree. But she was never satisfied with it. You'd see her glaring at it in the middle of the carol service.

I said teachers go crazy at Christmas time, but it seems to get headmistresses even worse. Ours went berserk. She charged round the school like a mad elephant, cursing and shouting at anybody who got in her way. The worst day was the one when she cooked a Christmas dinner for the teachers. She's the only person I know who cooks Christmas pudding in the lav! My mum won't believe me when I tell her. If you were sent to Mrs. Foster for anything on that day, she always asked you to look in her lav to see if the pudding was OK. One year, young Sylvia Thompson looked, and the pudding had boiled dry, but Sylvia was too scared to say so. Miss was having one of her long phone calls, shouting down the line at somebody, until the clouds of smoke reached her room. Sylvia was still waiting to see Miss, but when she heard the shout of rage when Miss saw the burnt mess in the pan, Sylvia ran for it. She didn't stop till she was home. She didn't even stop for her coat, even though it was snowing. And no way would she come to school again till the middle of January, even if she did miss the party and the concert. She stayed at home and played her piano all day instead.

When the tree was up it had to be decorated, and that meant a lot more arguing and shouting. Who said Christmas was a time of Good Will? Not in our school, it wasn't! No way.

It was the decorating of the tree that gave Don one of his best ideas.

"Let's have a live fairy," he said. "On top of the tree. For a laugh."

"Great!" said Mark.

"You could do it," said Darren. "It's your idea; you do it."

"Yeah!" said Mark.

"Right," said Don, "I will."

"You're joking," said Mark.

"I'm not," said Don. "I'm not. I'll do it. You'll see. And I know where we can get a fairy dress."

"Linda," said Darren. "She's got one. In her bag. I've seen it."

"You could do your dance," said Mark. "That'd be a real laugh."

I haven't told you about Don's dance. It's an Egyptian dance. A funny one. Like the ones they do in these old films. And Don is fat, very fat. He does his dance in PE. When Sir puts a record on and says, "Now follow the music. Just let it carry you along. Let the music tell you how to move," this is what Don always does; his Egyptian dance. It doesn't matter what the music is, he fits it in somehow. And it breaks everything up, because nobody can help laughing, not even Sir, no matter how cross he is. There's Don, in nothing but his underpants, because he's forgotten his PE things yet again, with his great belly sagging and wobbling and swinging about, tripping along on the tips of his toes, waving his arms to and fro, doing his Egyptian dance, with a silly sweet smile on his fat face.

"How could I do my dance at the top of the tree?" said Don.

"No, you could climb down and do it," said Darren. "In the middle of All Shepherds... We could say it was part of the concert. What a laugh!"

We waited till Sir was busy in the Hall with one of his "staff meetings," then Mark told Linda to get her fairy costume out.

"Who wants it?" said Linda in her snootiest voice.

"It's for me," said Don. "I'm going to be the fairy on the Christmas tree, and don't tell Sir or you'll get battered, see?"

Well, Linda knew, really, all the class knew, but she was pretending not to. She didn't want to lend her costume. You can't blame her, when you see Don. But she knew she'd have to give it up in the end, because all the class wanted to see Don dress up as a fairy and do his dance. It would be the biggest laugh ever. In the end, Darren and Mark had to twist Linda's arms before she would give them the costume. They didn't care about making her cry. That's the sort they are. I felt rotten not doing anything to stop them, but they'd only have beaten me up if I'd tried.

Don stripped down to his underpants, then tried to get Linda's fairy dress on. We should have known it wouldn't fit. It was miles too little for Don. He got half way in, then was stuck. Mark and Darren pulled at the dress until there was a ripping sound, and it came apart at the seams. Linda was crying and shouting, "My mum'll kill me! She spent hours making that dress!" but they took no notice.

In the end, they tore the wings off the dress, and stuck them on Don's back with sellotape. Then they made a veil to go over his face with the rest of the dress. Then he did his dance round the classroom, and we all fell out of our desks with laughing. All except Linda. She sat in the library corner, and went on crying by herself.

The next thing was to see if Don could climb up the Christmas tree.

"Sir'll be back soon. We'll do it at playtime," said Don.

Don got dressed again, and Mark stuffed the bits of the fairy costume behind a radiator, and when Sir came back we were all sitting at our tables reading.

"Well done," he said. "I'm pleased that you can enjoy your books sensibly whilst I'm busy with a staff meeting in the Hall. You can all go out early for playtime for being so helpful."

I was last one out, and Sir said to me, "Why is Linda crying in the book-corner?"

He went to cheer her up, and ask her what was wrong, but she just pushed him away.

"What's been going on?" he said to me.

"Don't know, Sir. Nothing, Sir," I said.

Well, I couldn't tell, could I?

Sir went off to the staff-room. We knew he'd be a long time, because all the teachers were having a booze-up for Christmas. Darren had seen Mrs. Gulam bringing the box of glasses from the stock-room that morning. We went back to the classroom, and Don got changed again into his fairy get up. Then Darren got his coat from the cloakroom, and covered Don with it. We got to the Hall without anybody seeing us. We met our Timmy on the way, with three more kids from the infants, and they ran up to us, shouting, "What are you doing?"

We had to give them a toffee each to go away and keep quiet.

We got to the Hall, and Don took the coat off. He did a quick twirl of his dance round the empty Hall; he couldn't resist it. This started us off laughing again.

"Come on, get on with it," said Darren. "You'll have somebody catching us. Get up that tree, Don."

Don went up to the tree. It was a very big one, and Sir had wedged it firmly in a dustbin, with lumps of concrete to weight it down. It looked solid enough. But Don hadn't bargained for the pine-needles being so tickly and prickly. As soon as they touched his belly, he yelped and jumped a few inches in the air.

"Go on, don't be soft," said Mark. "Get on with it."

Don tried again. He screwed his face up, and made a rush at the tree. He grabbed at the trunk and began to climb. Ugh! I was glad it wasn't me. He was scratched all over, and the needles went in his eyes and even up his nose. You must say he had a good try, though. He struggled about half way up, then the tree began to groan and creak.

Suddenly, he must have passed the balancing place, because the tree and the dustbin it stood in tipped over together, and crashed down with Don underneath! Wow, what a yell he made! He couldn't get out, and the needles were pressing into his fat flesh. I think its the only time I ever felt really sorry for Don. He wriggled like mad, but that only made it worse. We all heaved at the tree, and lifted it far enough for him to crawl out. What a sight he was! And there wasn't much left of the fairy costume.

"Run!" shouted Naseem, "Sir's coming!"

16
On With the Dance

We got away just in time, but we didn't have time to stand the tree up. We could hear Sir in the distance shouting at some little kids who happened to be passing on the way to the bogs, asking them who had knocked the tree over. But they wouldn't know what he was on about. We hid the remains of the fairy costume, and went out into the playground to plan our next step. Linda came up and asked for her costume, but Don said, "Don't worry about that. It's quite safe with us."

"But I need it for the concert," she wailed, "and my mum spent hours making it. Hours and hours."

"Get lost!" said Mark, and she went away, sniffing.

"I know," said Darren, "I'll get my sister to mend the costume. She'll not mind. She can do it tonight."

Various scraps of cloth and pieces of fairy's wings were smuggled out that night, under coats and in duffel-bags.

"The problem is," said Mumtaz, the next day, "that Don is really too, er, well . . . you know . . . too . . ."

"Too fat," said Mark, who could easily beat Don in a fight.

"Yes," said Mumtaz. "Too *large* to climb the tree. What we need is somebody real small."

"What about my dance," said Don.

"You could still do it," said Mumtaz. "You could hide

under the stage, and come out to do your dance when we give you a signal."

"Well, who could go up the tree?" said Don. "Who's the smallest in the class?"

Everybody looked at Jimmy.

"Not me!" said Jimmy.

"*YES!*" we all said.

"You'll have to do it, Jimmy," said Don, "because I'll batter you if you don't. Anyway, you'll like being a fairy. You'll be able to fly when you go outside, where there's a lot of room. You'll be able to zoom over the chimney-pots and meet Father Christmas."

Jimmy would believe almost anything you told him, specially if he wanted to. The idea of flying seemed great to him, so he believed it.

"Now we'll need two fairy-costumes," said Darren.

"I can get one," said Mumtaz. "My sister has one, and she's about Jimmy's size."

"Can she fly in it?" said Jimmy, eagerly.

"Oh, yes," said Mumtaz." She goes out every night. Haven't you seen her flying over Asda?"

"Yes. Yes, that's right," said Jimmy.

He's a right nutter, that boy.

We had a right old time getting Jimmy into that fairy-costume. He kept on wanting to go out and try his wings. They were very nice wings, you had to admit. Jimmy looked like a deformed fly when it was on. It was a good thing that Sir was so busy with his pantomime, or else he would have noticed what we were up to, for sure.

At last, we found a time when we could get into the Hall without anyone seeing, and we got Jimmy up the tree as well. He isn't much bigger than an infant, so he was light enough for the tree to hold him. Besides, Sir had fixed the tree even more carefully after it had fallen down. The needles gave Jimmy a good scratching, but he went up, helped on by threats of murder from below, and he got near the top, where there was a thick branch that he could sit on.

"That'll do, Jimmy," said Don. "Sit still on that branch. Then, when they're all in the Hall on concert night, and it's all quiet, you can give them a fright."

Jimmy loved being up in the tree, and we had a hard job

to get him to come down.

You know, I never thought Don would get away with it. I know it was a big tree, but surely someone would see Jimmy sitting there long before everyone had come into the Hall? But the funny thing is that once the tree's been there for a week, nobody really looks at it. They've got so used to it, that it's like part of the furniture.

It was awful getting Jimmy into the Hall before the carol concert. Four of us had to hide under the stage with him, to make sure he didn't run away or change his mind, and then come out when nobody was about. Of course, the tree had its lights and ornaments on by then, and when Jimmy climbed it they clinked and jingled like bells. Quite a few fell, like ripe fruit, and smashed on the floor, and Mark had to go for a dustpan to sweep them up.

Everyone was in position at last. Jimmy in the top of the tree. Don under the stage. Both in fairy costumes. The rest of us went off to get ready for the concert. I noticed that the tree was shaking, and a sound of giggling was coming from it. I went back and whispered up to Jimmy, "Stop it! Keep still and shush!"

That only made him worse, so I left him to it.

"What if he gets cramp?" said Alice.

"Too bad," I said. "It's too late to think of that."

I must say we all felt very nervous as we went into the Hall for the carol service. Most of Jimmy was well hidden by the thick branches of the tree, but you could quite clearly see a foot and part of his leg. But the teachers were too busy fussing about getting us sitting in the right places to notice the tree, and the kids were too busy looking out for Father Christmas arriving with his presents. So nobody noticed.

But, when everybody was settled, and all was quiet, and the vicar was ready to speak, there was something that you couldn't miss noticing. Well, two things. One was a strange snorting sound coming from under the stage. The other was that the tree was shaking. Very odd. Not to us. We knew only too well. They were going to give the show away too soon. Don had dropped off to sleep under the stage, and now he was snoring gently. Jimmy had started his silent giggling in the tree, and was making it tremble as though a storm was on the way. True, a storm was on the way. You could see Mrs. Foster twitching her nose and glaring round suspiciously. She whispered in Sir's ear, and he had to get his hanky to wipe it dry.

Now Sir began to look all over the Hall, and his eyes rested on the tree. The vicar was old and deaf and short-sighted, and he seemed not to have noticed anything odd. He went on with his speech. Sir looked puzzled. Very puzzled. He had seen Jimmy's foot. He'd been suspicious ever since getting notes to say that Don and Jimmy would not be able to come to the carol service because both had colds. They had never missed before, no matter how ill they were. It was strange, too, that these two had colds at the same time. But Jimmy was often absent for other reasons, like going for a haircut or for new shoes, so Sir didn't do anything about the notes. Now he crept up to me, bent down and whispered in my ear. "Who is that in the tree?"

"Don't know, Sir," I whispered.

"Oh, come on. I think you do. Is it Jimmy?"

I was getting a wet ear now. "Yes, Sir."

"What is he doing?"

I didn't have time to tell him. The tree shook more and more, and there was a sound of cracking branches and falling ornaments. An infant began crying. Two more joined in. Jimmy's face appeared, for an instant, at the top of the tree, and he shouted, "Hello, everybody!"

Then he appeared to spread his wings, as though he meant to fly round the Hall. With a whoosh, he fell out of the tree. I've never seen anyone move so fast as Miss Edwards at that moment. In a flash, she was under the tree, with her arms stretched out. She was a big lady. Big and soft, like a cushion. She looked as though you could bounce on her, like a trampoline. She caught Jimmy, and they both collapsed in a heap on the floor.

There was a rush of noise. Most of the kids were laughing. The grown-ups were going "oooooh," and "oh." Mrs. Foster was getting her temper up, and beginning to shout orders. All this wakened Don, and he thought he had missed the signal for him to come out from under the stage. Out he came, and stood blinking in the light, in the middle of all this commotion. Naseem switched on the cassette we had got ready, with the Egyptian dance on it, and Don sprang into action. He shimmied round the hall,

with his belly wobbling as it had never wobbled before. He was a sensation! He really was. He brought the house down! (I never knew what that meant, but I know now). Everybody was so flabbergasted that they stood and watched him for what seemed ages. Then Mrs. Foster bellowed, "*STOP!!!!*" and everything froze.

"Turn that music off."

Naseem stopped the tape.

Oh dear. What a row there was. I thought it would never end. What a fuss. It was only a joke.

The row went on for days. Parents were sent for. But it was Christmas. The vicar was a good sport.

"It's Christian to forgive," he said, when he came to see us. "And, specially as it is Christmas, you are forgiven."

Then he started telling us about the things he did when he was a kid, and Mrs. Foster hurried him away as soon as she could, for a cup of tea in her room.

We had a good laugh about it after, though. That was one of the best Christmasses ever, in our school.

17
End of Term

The teachers' pantomime was super. It was "Sleeping Beauty," as I already knew, but I had to pretend to be as surprised as everyone else. It's amazing how well the secret was kept. Secrets are usually impossible in school if more than one person knows them.

Sir always had a leading part. But there's something weird about our Sir, because, every year, in the panto, he arranges to have an egg broken over his head, or a custard tart thrown at him. He seems to enjoy it. Then he turns up in the classroom, after, with his hair looking clean but wet. I know his secret. He goes in the staff bogs for a quick shampoo. I saw him with it in his hand one year.

But it was a great pantomime, and Mrs. Bell made a lovely Sleeping Beauty. I think Mumtaz fell in love with her; I've never seen him looking so soppy. Mrs. Foster was the wicked witch, and she was just right for the part. She didn't really need to act at all. She only had to be herself. My mum said that was called "type-casting," but she wouldn't explain what she meant.

After that business with the Christmas tree, Don gave the remains of her fairy-costume back to Linda, and Mumtaz gave her what was left of his sister's costume as well. Then Sir said, "You should be able to make one good costume out of two damaged ones, Linda. Now you don't need to do any jobs for me, and you can stay in whenever you like at playtime, and it should be ready in time for the concert."

"Can Alice stay in with me?" said Linda.

"All right, then."

Lucky Linda! While we were shivering in the icy playground, that last week of term, she and Alice were all cosy in the classroom. They set up a workshop in the reading-corner, and nobody was allowed near. Well, it made up a bit for having her costume messed about by Don.

The school concert came right at the end of term, on the Wednesday. That left Thursday and Friday for clearing up for the end of term. Our dress rehearsal was on the Tuesday, and Linda did her fairy dance. She had done a marvellous job with the costume, but it did seem a bit loose in places. She was good at sewing, but not so good at maths. Sir said, "Are you sure you've measured yourself properly, Linda?"

"Yes, Sir, course I have."

"Well, I think you'd better make a quick check this afternoon."

I don't think Linda was listening properly, because Alice was whispering in her ear at the same time. Anyway, she did this dance, with a lot of jumping about, and nothing fell off, so it didn't seem too bad.

"Can I do my dance again?" said Don.

I think he thought that his dance hadn't been properly done on the night of the carol concert. He had been stopped too soon to get really going.

"Definitely not!" said Sir.

"Well can I do my Laurel and Hardy act with Mark?"

"Yes, that would be much better."

So they practised that at the rehearsal, and Sir said it was really good.

The night of the concert came, and all the parents came donned up in their best clothes. The infants did their nativity play, as they did every year, and our Timmy, being so little, was baby Jesus. He had to lie in a laundry-basket full of straw from the craft-box, wearing nothing but a baby's nappy. The straw tickled him, and he kept

laughing, so that spoilt the effect a bit. I mean, you don't think of Jesus laughing when the wise men come to see him, do you?

Don and Mark did the Laurel and Hardy act, and it was very funny. The audience really enjoyed it. But there was a surprise at the end of this act. Hardy did a quick striptease, and there he was, a fairy once more! Where on earth had he got another costume? There was nothing Sir could do to stop him. The Egyptian music started up (Sir had a word with Naseem the next day), and Don pranced all round the Hall. There was one extra touch. He had filled his belly-button with glitter. (It took months to get it all out). This made the quivering of his belly all the more funny, and even Mrs. Foster had to laugh. He was a great success.

Then the choir sang a carol, and Naseem and Dipali did a Pakistani dance, to a tape Naseem's dad brought back last time he went for a holiday. They wore their best saris, all glittering with gold thread. It was lovely. It made Don's dance look more daft than ever.

There was another play, about gnomes, from the Top Infants, and at last it was time for Linda's fairy dance. Somehow, coming after Don's fairy dance, Linda's wasn't the same. The audience didn't know whether it was meant to be another funny dance or not. After a while, they decided it wasn't funny, and wiped the grins off their faces, as Linda did her ballet steps across the stage. It did go on a bit, with various jumps and fancy bits where she did the splits. It wasn't really part of the dance, but I reckon she'd learnt how to do it, and wanted to show off. I think it was the splits, though, that caused her downfall. That and the fact that the costume didn't fit properly. You could see it looked a bit baggy in places. Not quite right for a fairy.

All the time Linda was dancing, Alice was waiting at the back in her ballet gear, because the two of them were going to dance together to finish off. You could see Alice peeping through a gap in the scenery. There was a bit where Linda was doing a lot of bending over, and the music went quiet. Suddenly, in the middle of this hush, there was a loud whisper from Alice. She must have thought nobody could hear her, but everybody could. She said, 'I can see your bum."

Everything froze. Linda had turned into a statue, and the music went on without her. Then, as she began to

shuffle sideways across the stage, we all saw her knickers
drop to her knees, then to her ankles. She held her short
skirt down in front of her with her hands, and stepped
daintily out of her knickers. Then she kicked them into
touch at the side of the stage, and continued her sideways
shuffle until she disappeared behind the scenery. It had
taken Sir till now to get to the switches, and he knocked all
the lights off. In the dark you could hear Alice and Linda
whispering together, and then a howl of laughter from
the audience covered up any other sound.

Alice grabbed a blanket off an infant shepherd, leaving
him shivering in his underpants, and wrapped it round

Linda, and they ran to the classroom.

There should have been another act in the concert, but the audience was laughing too much to settle down to anything. So Mrs. Foster told everyone not to be silly, said thank you to all who had helped with the concert, and sent us home early. On the way out, I heard her say to Don, "I'll see you tomorrow, young man. First thing."

Mrs. Foster didn't see Don the next day, as he stayed off for the rest of the week, and then it was the holidays. We didn't see Alice and Linda either, as they did the same. Well, I don't know why they were so bothered. It was only Alice that saw Linda's bum, and everybody's seen a pair of knickers before. You can see thousands of them in Marks and Sparks. I don't really know why knickers are so funny. You only have to say "knickers" in our school, to start the whole class laughing. Try saying "underpants" and nobody would even smile. They'd think you were bonkers if you laughed at that.

After that, we had two days of tidying up. It was like a flitting. Everything had to come down. All the displays. All the Christmas decorations. All the term's work and the work Sir had put up for Parents' Evening. The lot. And all our books were packed away. It looked awful when we had finished. All bare and dead. But Sir kept his books of games and puzzles out, so we had some fun on the last afternoon. Mumtaz shouted, "Three cheers for Sir!" and we all cheered as loudly as we could. Some of the kids gave Sir a present, all wrapped up in fancy paper, and wished him a Merry Christmas, and it was time to go home.

Then it was the Christmas holidays, with shopping to do and cards to write, and letters to Father Christmas. But we'd all be back in January.

PS. Mumtaz has just read this, and he says I didn't tell how Sir's trousers got on fire. It was during that pantomime. Sir had changed into his pantomime costume, and left his trousers in the staff-room. He sent Mark to get them, and told him to hang them up near the Christmas tree. Mark hung them too near to the tree, because there was a crib under it, with a lot of candles on it that Mrs. Foster had lit without telling Sir. The trousers didn't blaze up, but the candles melted a big hole in them, and Sir had to go home in his pantomime costume. I bet he felt silly.

I think that's everything. Bye!